Three Squeezes

For my entire family with squeezes innumerable —J.P.

Text copyright © 2020 by Jason Pratt
Illustrations copyright © 2020 by Chris Sheban
Published by Roaring Brook Press
Roaring Brook Press is a division of Holtzbrinck Publishing Holdings Limited Partnership
120 Broadway, New York, NY 10271
mackids.com

Library of Congress Control Number: 2019948842

ISBN 978-1-250-31345-4

Our books may be purchased in bulk for promotional, educational, or business use.
Please contact your local bookseller or the Macmillan Corporate and Premium Sales Department at (800) 221-7945 ext. 5442
or by email at MacmillanSpecialMarkets@macmillan.com.

First edition, 2020
Book design by Jen Keenan
Printed in China by RR Donnelley Asia Printing Solutions Ltd., Dongguan City, Guangdong Province

1 3 5 7 9 10 8 6 4 2

Three Squeezes

written by
JASON PRATT

illustrated by
CHRIS SHEBAN

ROARING BROOK PRESS
NEW YORK

When you could neither talk nor stand,

life's hourglass still filled with sand,

I gently held your tiny hand
and gave it *three soft squeezes.*

When you awoke within the night
and cried from fear and called for light,

I held you safe with all my might

and gave you *three long squeezes.*

When you fell down and skinned your knee

or tumbled from your climbing tree,

I pulled you tightly into me
and gave you *three firm squeezes.*

Through all the times you tried your best

and won a few but lost the rest,

I held you close against my chest

and gave you *three good squeezes*.

Though quarrels every now and then

gave both our hearts a need to mend,

I knew that healing would begin

by sharing *three strong squeezes*.

As days crept on and years flew by

(for days will creep and years will fly),

each tear-filled low and cheer-filled high

was met with *three more squeezes*.

Where you were once so small and frail,

you now stand tall, all set to sail.

And though you're not afraid to fail,

I'll wait with **countless squeezes**.

And one day when you're fully grown,

with home and family of your own,

I'll smile because I'll know I've shown

the meaning of *three squeezes*.

The day may come, you understand,

when I can neither talk nor stand,

and if it does, please take my hand

and give it **three soft squeezes**.

For as I aged and as you grew,

I know that you and I both knew

that I was saying "I love you"
by way of my *three squeezes*.